HIPPOS GO BERSERK!

WRITTEN AND ILLUSTRATED BY SANDRA BOYNTON

Aladdin Paperbacks

"*I* didn't invite them. Did *you* invite them?"
(For Mom and Dad, with love.)

LITTLE SIMON

An imprint of Simon & Schuster Children's Publishing Division
1230 Avenue of the Americas, New York, New York 10020
Copyright © 1977, 1996 by Sandra Boynton
Copyright renewed © 2005 by Sandra K. Boynton
All rights reserved, including the right of reproduction in whole or in part in any form.
LITTLE SIMON is a registered trademark of Simon & Schuster, Inc., and associated
colophon is a trademark of Simon & Schuster, Inc.
For information about special discounts for bulk purchases, please contact Simon &
Schuster Special Sales at 1-866-506-1949 or business@simonandschuster.com.
The Simon & Schuster Speakers Bureau can bring authors to your live event. For more
information or to book an event contact the Simon & Schuster Speakers Bureau at 1-866-
248-3049 or visit our website at www.simonspeakers.com.
The text of this book was set in Times Roman.
Manufactured in China
LCCN: 96-84706
ISBN 978-0-689-80854-8
ISBN 978-1-4169-9619-4 (unjacketed edition)

One hippo, all alone,

1

calls two hippos

on the phone.

3

Three hippos at the door

bring along another four.

Five hippos come overdressed.

5

Six hippos show up with a guest.

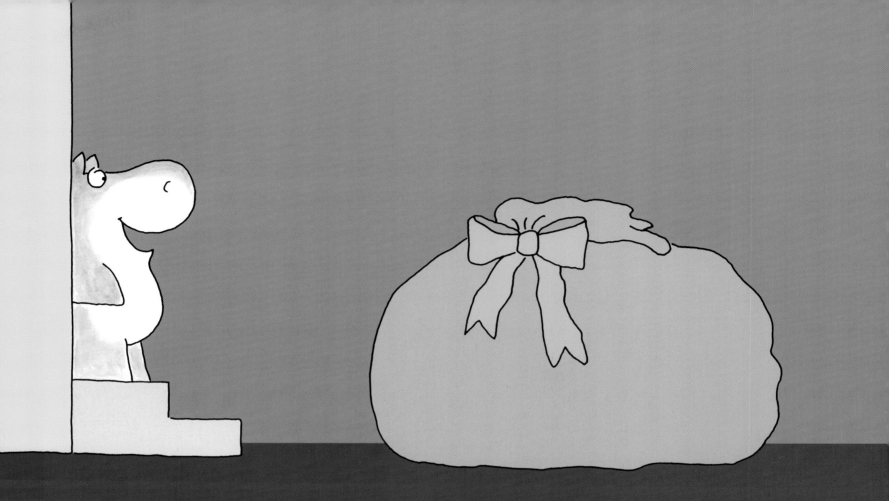

Seven hippos

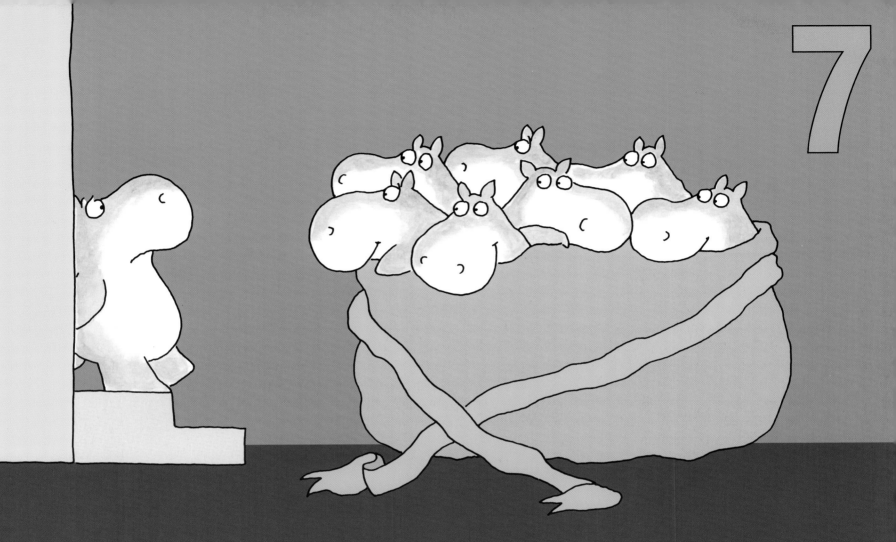

arrive in a sack.

8

Eight hippos
sneak in the back.

Nine hippos

come to work.

ALL THE HIPPOS

All through the hippo night,
hippos play with great delight.

But at the hippo break of day,
the hippos all must go away.

9

Nine hippos and a beast join

eight hippos riding east, while

seven hippos moving west leave

six hippos quite distressed, and

five hippos then set forth with

four hippos headed north.

Three hippos say, "Good day."

The last two hippos go their way.

One hippo, alone once more,

misses the other forty-four.